THE AMAZING A to Z THING

by Sally Morgan   illustrated by Bronwyn Bancroft

LITTLE HARE
www.littleharebooks.com

A

is for
Anteater

Anteater had something **amazing** to show her friends.

She invited Bilby to take a look.

B

is for
Bilby

'It will make you gasp in astonishment, Bilby,'
said Anteater.

But Bilby was too busy resting. 'Show Chuditch,' he said.

C

is for
Chuditch

`I have something to make you squeal with happiness, Chuditch,` said Anteater.

But Chuditch was too busy smiling at herself in the water. `Show Dingo,` she said.

D is for Dingo

'I have something to fascinate you, Dingo,' said Anteater.

But Dingo was too busy rolling in the dirt. 'Shoo Emu,' he said.

E is for Emu

'I have something for you to celebrate, Emu,' said Anteater. But Emu was too busy standing on one leg. 'Show Flying Fox,' she said.

F

is for
Flying
Fox

'I have something to make you shout with joy, Flying Fox,' said Anteater. But Flying Fox was too busy scratching his ears.

'Shou Galah,' he said.

G is for **Galah**

'I have something to make you dance, Galah,' said Anteater. But Galah was too busy gossiping with her friends. 'Show Huntsman Spider,' she said.

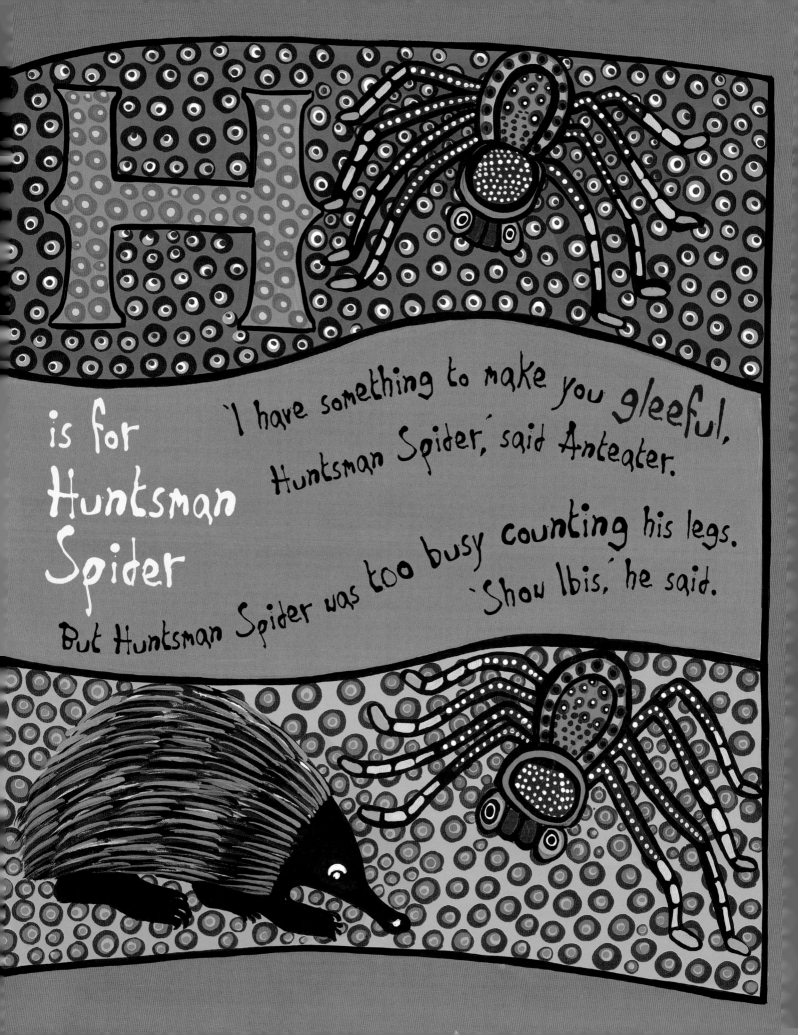

H

is for
Huntsman
Spider

'I have something to make you gleeful, Huntsman Spider,' said Anteater.

But Huntsman Spider was too busy counting his legs. 'Shoo Ibis,' he said.

is for
Ibis

`I have something to enchant you, Ibis,´ said Anteater.

But Ibis was too busy washing her feet.
`Show Jellyfish´, she said.

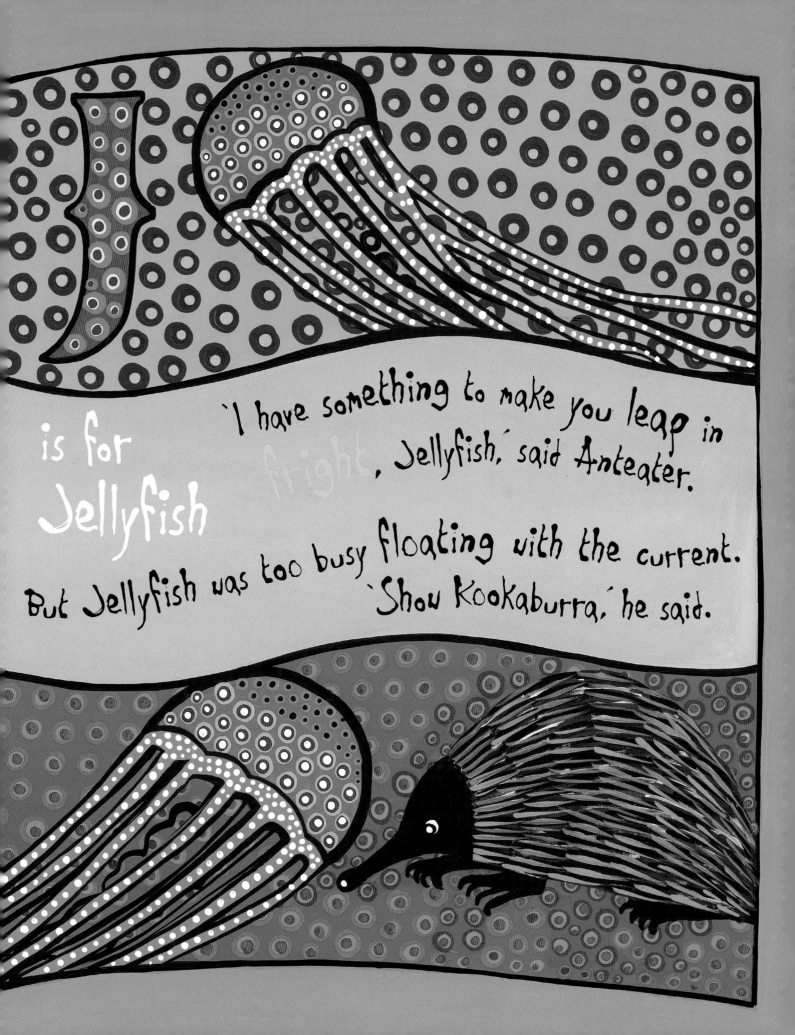

J is for Jellyfish

'I have something to make you leap in fright, Jellyfish,' said Anteater.

But Jellyfish was too busy floating with the current. 'Show Kookaburra,' he said.

K is for Kookaburra

'I have something to make your head *spin*, Kookaburra,' said Anteater.

But Kookaburra was too busy having a snooze.

'Show Lizard,' he said.

L is for **Lizard**

'I have something to make you giggle, Lizard,' said Anteater.

But Lizard was too busy chewing his claws.
'Show Magpie,' he said.

M

is for Magpie

'I have something to make you sing with pleasure, Magpie,' said Anteater. But Magpie was too busy scratching a spot. 'Show Numbat,' she said.

is for
Numbat

'I have something to make you jolly, Numbat,' said Anteater.

But Numbat was too busy watching grass grow. 'Show Owl,' he said.

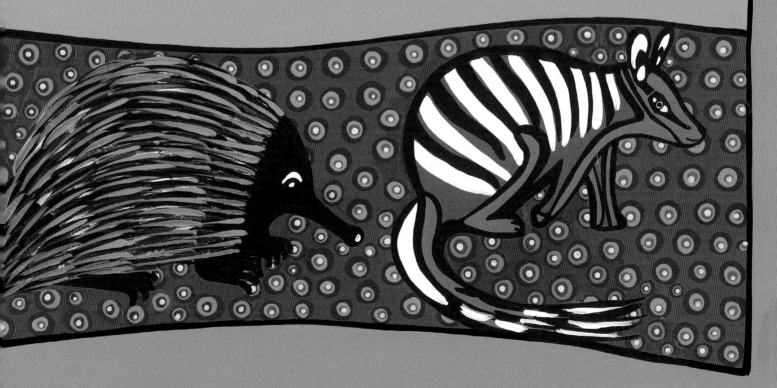

O is for **Owl**

'I have something to make you hoot, Owl,' said Anteater. But Owl was too busy fluffing his feathers. 'Show Python,' he said.

P is for Python

`I have something to make you laugh, Python,' said Anteater.

But Python was too busy lying in the sun. `Show Quokka,' she said.

is for
Quokka

'I have something to rattle you, Quokka,' said Anteater.

But Quokka was too busy lying in the shade. 'Show Rat,' she said.

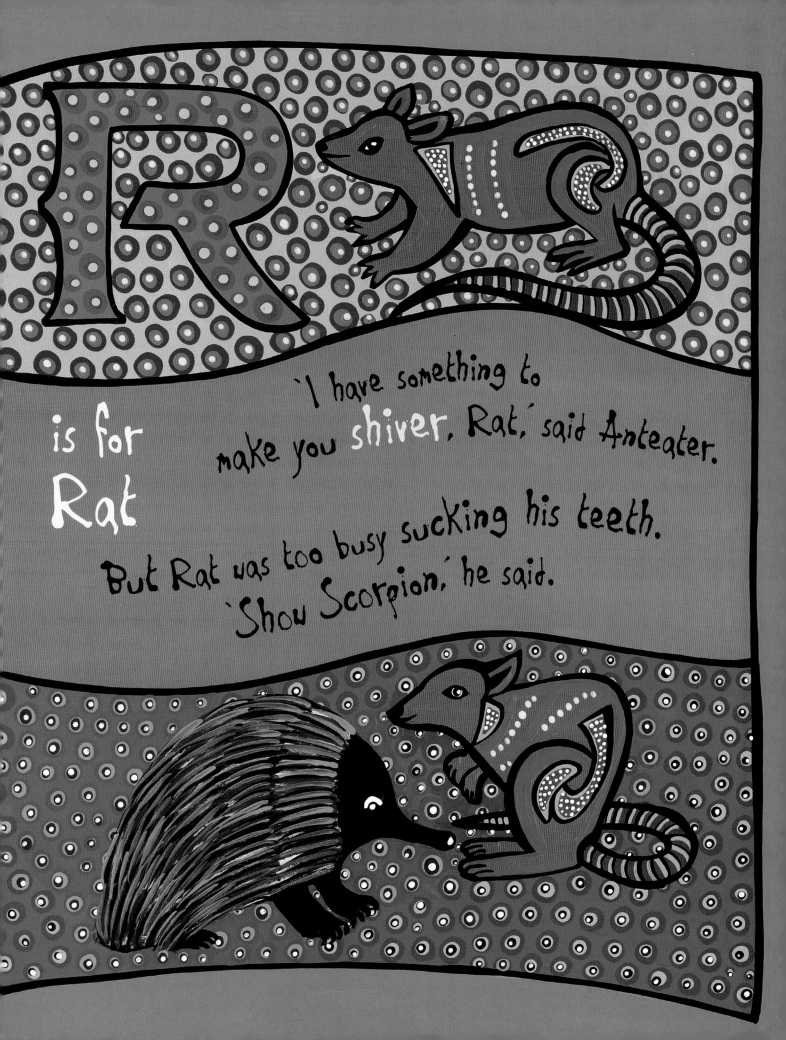

R is for Rat

'I have something to make you shiver, Rat,' said Anteater.

But Rat was too busy sucking his teeth. 'Show Scorpion,' he said.

S

is for Scorpion

'I have something to make you cackle, Scorpion,' said Anteater.

But Scorpion was too busy staring at the sky.

'Show Turtle,' she said.

is for Turtle

'I have something to make you quiver, Turtle,' said Anteater.

But Turtle was too busy thinking about lunch. 'Show Ulysses Butterfly,' he said.

U is for Ulysses Butterfly

'I have something to make you feel brave, Ulysses Butterfly,' said Anteater.

But Ulysses Butterfly was too busy hovering in the air. 'Show Velvet Worm,' she said.

is for
Velvet
Worm

'I have something to delight you, Velvet Worm,' said Anteater.

But Velvet Worm was too busy tying himself in knots.

'Show Wallaby,' he said.

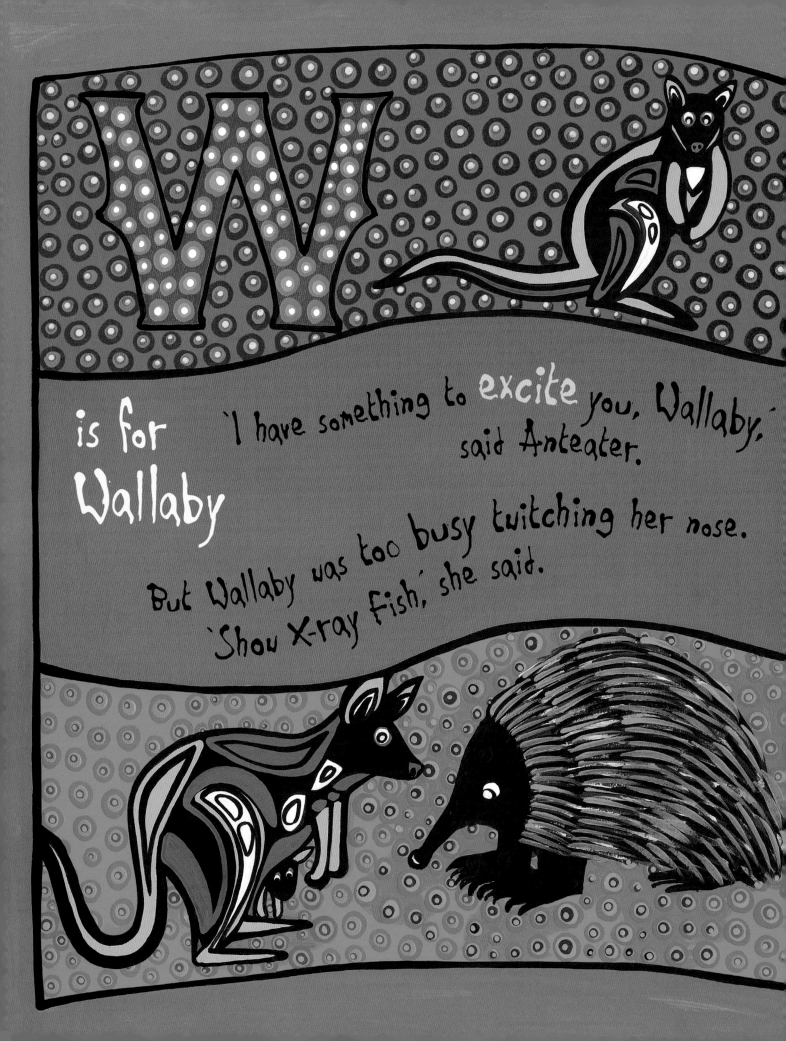

W

is for
Wallaby

`I have something to excite you, Wallaby,`
said Anteater.

But Wallaby was too busy twitching her nose.
`Show X-ray Fish,` she said.

X

is for
X-ray
Fish

'I have something to make you **wonder**, X-ray Fish,' said Anteater.

But X-ray Fish was too busy blowing bubbles. 'Show Yabby,' he said.

Y is for Yabby

'I have something to make you zing, Yabby,' said Anteater.

But Yabby was too busy yawning.
'Shoo Zebra Finch,' she said.

Z is for
Zebra
Finch

`I have something to make you chirp with **surprise**, Zebra Finch,' said Anteater.

But Zebra Finch was too busy snoring ...

'Well,' said Anteater,
'I'll look at it myself.'

So she opened it,
and she gasped and giggled

and hooted and laughed
and shouted and danced
and cackled and rattled and shivered
and wondered
and had so much fun...

that all the other animals suddenly discovered
they weren't too busy to have a look